MIXED MARTIAL ARTS

MMA: HEROIC HISTORY

Frazer Andrew Krohn

Abdo & Daughters
MIDDLE GRADE NONFICTION
An imprint of Abdo Publishing
abdobooks.com

ABDOBOOKS.COM

Published by Abdo Publishing, a division of ABDO, PO Box 398166, Minneapolis, Minnesota 55439. Copyright © 2023 by Abdo Consulting Group, Inc. International copyrights reserved in all countries. No part of this book may be reproduced in any form without written permission from the publisher. Abdo & Daughters™ is a trademark and logo of Abdo Publishing.

102022
012023

THIS BOOK CONTAINS RECYCLED MATERIALS

Design: Kelly Doudna, Mighty Media, Inc.
Production: Mighty Media, Inc.
Editor: Liz Salzmann
Cover Photograph: Anton_Ivanov/Shutterstock Images
Interior Photographs: A.RICARDO/Shutterstock Images, pp. 29, 44 (top, bottom), 49 (left), 54–55, 56; Aflo Co. Ltd./Alamy Photo, p. 14; Andre Luiz Moreira/Shutterstock Images, pp. 41, 46; Andrius Petrucenia/Wikimedia Commons, p. 15; Anthony Nesmith/AP Images, p. 48 (bottom); Arquivo Nacional Collection/Wikimedia Commons, p. 13; Art Davie/Wikimedia Commons, p. 28 (top); Cassiano Correia/Shutterstock Images, pp. 26–27; Eric Jamison/AP Images, pp. 37, 61 (bottom left); Etsuo Hara/Getty Images, pp. 34, 52; fightlaunch/Flickr, p. 7; FPS CORP/Wikimedia Commons, p. 21; Isaac Brekken/AP Images, p. 57; Kathy Hutchins/Shutterstock Images, pp. 47 (bottom), 49 (right); Kobby Dagan/Shutterstock Images, p. 6; LAURA RAUCH/AP Images, p. 38; Louis Grasse/PxImages/AP Images, p. 35; Louis Grasse/PxImages/Icon Sportswire/AP Images, p. 59; Markus Boesch/Getty Images, pp. 24–25, 31; Matthew Tosh/Wikimedia Commons, pp. 47 (top), 61 (top right); MD/AP Images, pp. 23, 60 (top); Meidosensei/Wikimedia Commons, pp. 16, 60 (bottom right); Nox Yang/Image Press Agency/AP Images, p. 53 (top); PAOLO VILLA VERONA ITALY/Wikimedia Commons, pp. 8–9; PictureLux/The Hollywood Archive/Alamy Photo, p. 17; Piotr Drabik/Wikimedia Commons, p. 40; Prometheus72/Shutterstock Images, p. 28 (bottom); REUTERS/Alamy Photo, pp. 4–5; Sankei/Getty Images, p. 36; Stephen McCarthy/Web Summit via Sportsfile/Flickr, p. 48 (top); T photography/Shutterstock Images, pp. 18–19; TcoxPFL/Wikimedia Commons, pp. 50, 61 (bottom right); Tinseltown/Shutterstock Images, p. 39; Webitect/Shutterstock Images, p. 53 (bottom); Wikimedia Commons, pp. 10, 11, 19, 20, 22, 32–33, 45, 58, 60 (bottom left), 61 (top left); Wilfredo Lee/AP Images, pp. 42–43; YES Market Media/Shutterstock Images, p. 51; 079Doris/Wikimedia Commons, p. 30

Design Elements: Mighty Media, Inc.; mkirarslan/iStockphoto; sanchesnet1/iStockphoto

Library of Congress Control Number: 2022940773

Publisher's Cataloging-in-Publication Data

Names: Krohn, Frazer Andrew, author.
Title: MMA: heroic history / by Frazer Andrew Krohn
Description: Minneapolis, Minnesota : Abdo Publishing, 2023 | Series: Mixed martial arts | Includes online resources and index.
Identifiers: ISBN 9781532199226 (lib. bdg.) | ISBN 9781098274429 (ebook)
Subjects: LCSH: MMA (Mixed martial arts)--Juvenile literature. | Mixed martial arts--Juvenile literature. | Hand-to-hand fighting--Juvenile literature. | Ultimate fighting--Juvenile literature. | Sports--History--Juvenile literature.
Classification: DDC 796.81--dc23

CONTENTS

Griffin vs. Bonnar 5
Combat Origins 9
Early MMA Fights 19
MMA Goes Mainstream 25
Rise in Popularity 33
Promotion Fusion 43
What the Future Holds 55
Timeline 60

Glossary 62
Online Resources 63
Index 64

Griffin (*right*) and Bonnar met again in a UFC match in August 2006. It was close, with Griffin winning by judges' decision.

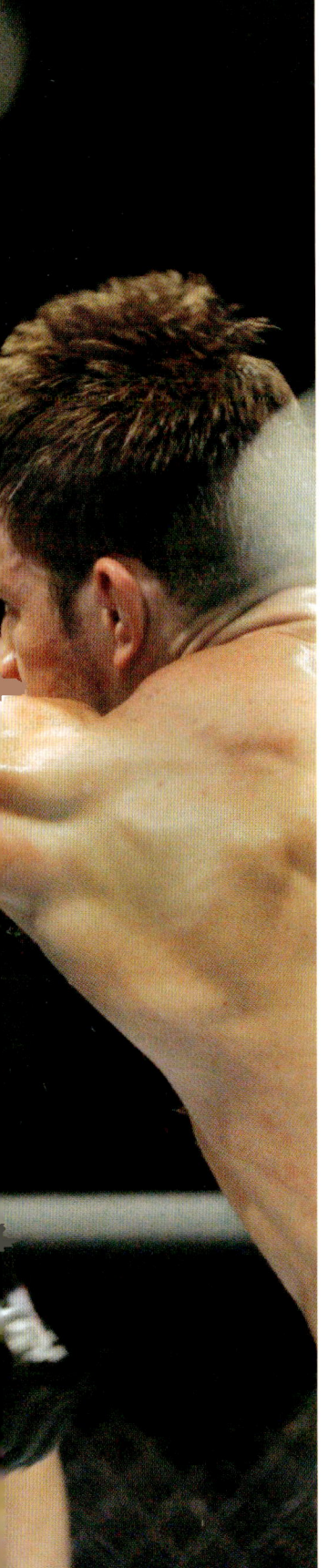

CHAPTER 1

GRIFFIN VS. BONNAR

"The most important fight in UFC history." These were the words of UFC president Dana White following the fight between Forrest Griffin and Stephan Bonnar on April 9, 2005. The bout is regarded as one of the most iconic fights not only in Ultimate Fighting Championship (UFC) history but also in mixed martial arts (MMA) history.

EPIC BATTLE

The fight, held in Las Vegas, Nevada, was the finale of *The Ultimate Fighter 1*, a reality television program that aired on Spike TV. Both Griffin and Bonnar were highly regarded during their time on *The Ultimate Fighter 1*. Fans expected a closely contested fight, and they were not disappointed. There were three five-minute rounds. This is the standard length for a non-title fight.

Forrest Griffin

    The fight started at a high pace. Griffin certainly got the upper hand in the first round, as commentator Joe Rogan stated. It was already beginning to heat up into an absolute classic. Following the standard one-minute break in between rounds, the two met again to throw down. After receiving a punch to the face, Bonnar cut Griffin's nose, causing the referee to stop the fight so the doctor could check the cut. Luckily for fans, the fight continued. Again, the two men met in the center and looked to unload on each other.

    In the third and final round, both men gave it their all, constantly looking to counter one another, landing shots at a distance and kicks to the body and legs, with takedowns mixed in too. After

15 action-packed minutes, the two men had no stamina left. Both were just hoping they'd done enough to have their hand raised at the end of the fight.

THE JUDGES WEIGH IN

All three judges scored the fight 29-28 in favor of Forrest Griffin. He won by just one point! As the winner of *The Ultimate Fighter 1*, Griffin received a contract to fight in the UFC from UFC president Dana White. But Bonnar's performance was so impressive that White also gave him a UFC contract, even though he lost. During the fight, the two men threw a total of 349 strikes. They put the UFC on the world stage, but none of this would have been possible without those who came before them.

Stephan Bonnar

Pankration was a common theme in ancient Greek pottery and art.

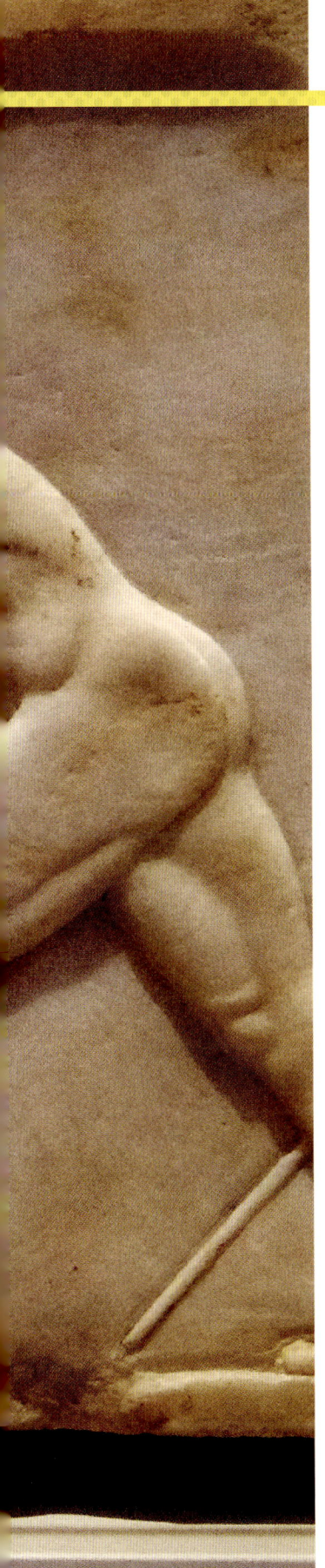

CHAPTER 2

COMBAT ORIGINS

Hand-to-hand combat dates back to ancient Greece. Long before stadiums full of fans watched modern-day MMA, the Greeks competed in pankration. The word *pankration* is a combination of the Greek words *pan*, meaning "all," and *kratos*, meaning "powers."

Pankration began as an Olympic sport in 648 BCE. It was a mix of striking and wrestling. The only rules were no biting and no eye-gouging. Fights would end only when one competitor was physically unable to continue, was forced to submit by their opponent, or was dead.

BEYOND GREECE

Originally, pankration competitors fought nude. Then the Romans adopted pankration, and Roman fighters wore loincloths. Fighters also wore battle gloves, known as *caesti*. These often were made of leather strips and filled with iron plates, blades, and sometimes spikes! We can

Kanō (*right*) with his star student Kyuzo Mifune. Many believe Mifune was the second-best judo practitioner ever, after Kanō.

see similarities with today's modern mixed martial arts, with competitors wearing slightly padded fingerless gloves when competing.

Hand-to-hand combat wasn't being practiced only in Europe. Asian martial arts including jiu-jitsu, judo, and karate came to light as effective methods of self-defense. Martial arts also developed in South America. The most important form was Brazilian jiu-jitsu (BJJ). BJJ is based on ground fighting, submissions, and controlling an opponent's power and momentum and using it against them.

Mitsuyo Maeda

FROM JAPAN TO BRAZIL

In 1882, Japanese jiu-jitsu practitioner Jigorō Kanō used principles of jiu-jitsu to found a new martial art called judo. One of Kanō's students, Mitsuyo Maeda, was sent to other countries to spread knowledge, impart wisdom, and demonstrate how effective their martial art could be. He taught people such as wrestlers, boxers, and street fighters how to use the correct techniques to throw opponents, manipulate their weight, and control them. There was also a focus on mental discipline, an element that has continued through to today's competition.

FIGHTIN' WORDS

Here are some common terms used in MMA.

FIGHT CARD // a program or list of the matches during an MMA event. The card usually has one or two headline, or main, matches plus several warm-up, or preliminary, matches.

GRAPPLE // to fight using throws, takedowns, holds, and other wrestling moves rather than punches or kicks.

KNOCKOUT (KO) // when one fighter has been knocked down and is unable to get up and resume fighting within a specified time.

ROUND // one of the periods of time a fight is divided into. MMA fights have three or five five-minute rounds with a one-minute rest between each round.

STRIKE // a blow delivered to an opponent while standing. A strike can be made by a fist, knee, elbow, or foot.

SUBMISSION // when a fighter wins by grabbing their opponent in a painful hold that they can't break free of, so that they are forced to give up.

TAKEDOWN // a move that forces or knocks an opponent to the ground.

TAP OUT // when a fighter taps the mat with their hand to indicate that they want to give up.

TECHNICAL KNOCKOUT (TKO) // when a fight referee stops a match because one of the fighters is too injured to continue.

Brazilian fighter Carlos Gracie attended a Kanō seminar in 1917. He was instantly hooked. Following years of training, learning, and improving under Maeda, Gracie passed his knowledge on to his brothers, in particular Hélio Gracie. Hélio was a short man, so it was difficult for him to use the throws of judo effectively. Therefore, he had to develop a way of manipulating his opponent's weight in his favor.

The Gracie brothers focused more on the ground fighting aspects of judo. They slowly but surely developed their own mixed martial art. They used the techniques of judo to create new movements and effective submission holds to immobilize opponents.

Hélio Gracie

Rickson Gracie (*top*) and Yuki Nakai competing at the Vale Tudo Japan tournament in 1995

The key aspect is to use an opponent's size and strength against them. The Gracie brothers' martial art came to be known as Brazilian jiu-jitsu (BJJ).

VALE TUDO

Vale Tudo became popular in Brazil during the twentieth century. It was an informal competition between those practicing different martial arts. Fighters would face off to determine whose martial art was more effective. The Gracie family was known to organize infamous "Gracie Challenge" Vale Tudo events. At them, anyone could challenge a member of the family. In this way, the Gracie family proved how effective and dangerous their BJJ was.

The name *Vale Tudo* is Portuguese for "everything goes" or "everything allowed." The style is also known as "no holds barred." Modern-day MMA is essentially Vale Tudo combined with BJJ.

Vale Tudo really was the beginning of MMA, as it pitted fighters from alternative, established martial arts against one another. Kickboxers would face wrestlers; boxers would face jiu-jitsu fighters. More often than not, those who practiced BJJ prevailed.

THE GODFATHER OF MMA

Bruce Lee is widely considered the godfather of modern MMA. Born in San Francisco, California, on November 27, 1940, he was a philosopher, actor, director, screenwriter, and producer. But most importantly, he was a martial artist. During the late 1960s and early 1970s, Lee developed his system of martial arts known as Jeet

Dana White

Kune Do. Jeet Kune Do focuses on using the easiest way to attack an opponent, without wasting motion or time. Jeet Kune Do draws on principles from several martial arts.

Lee brought martial arts to the mainstream with his legendary films featuring martial arts fighting. These included *The Way of the Dragon*, *Fist of Fury*, *The Big Boss*, *Game of Death*, and *Enter the Dragon*, which is considered one of the best martial arts movies of all time. With the popularity of these movies and Lee himself, naturally there was a huge boom in people taking up martial arts.

UFC president Dana White described Lee as the father of mixed martial arts. He also stated, "I think the sport of mixed martial arts was started by Bruce Lee. Bruce Lee's movies, Bruce Lee's philosophies, just Bruce Lee's image alone is very powerful." Sadly, Lee died in 1973 when he just 32 years old.

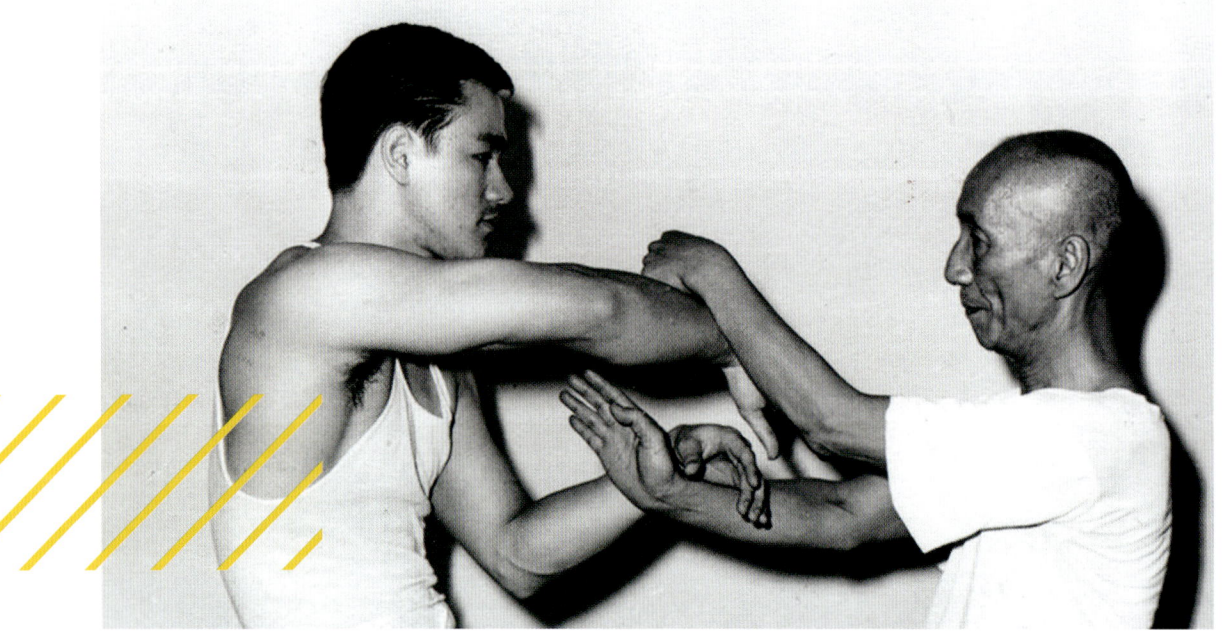

Lee (*left*) studied the martial art Wing Chun under grandmaster Ip Man (*right*).

Lee in the film *Enter the Dragon*

Maracanã Stadium opened in 1950. It is primarily used for soccer games.

CHAPTER 3

EARLY MMA FIGHTS

The Gracies would often promote their Gracie Challenge in local newspapers around Rio de Janeiro, Brazil. Their advertisements said, "If you want a broken arm or rib, contact Carlos Gracie." The goal of the matches was to prove that their martial art was superior to that of anyone else. Several of these matches became extremely famous at the time.

HÉLIO GRACIE VS. MASAHIKO KIMURA

This fight took place on October 23, 1951, at the Maracanã Stadium in Rio de Janeiro. Kimura defeated Hélio within 15 minutes. He broke Hélio's arm during the match while simultaneously

Masahiko Kimura

Kimura (*right*) studied under former all-Japan judo champion Tatsukuma Ushijima (*left*).

choking him unconscious. Carlos threw in the towel, and Kimura was declared the victor.

HÉLIO GRACIE VS. WALDEMAR SANTANA

In May 1955, Hélio was challenged to a Vale Tudo fight by a former pupil named Waldemar Santana. Hélio was much older and smaller than Santana. Still, Hélio held his own for more than three hours and 40 minutes. But he eventually tired, and Santana knocked him out with a soccer kick to the head. This marked Hélio's final match.

Carlson Gracie in 1999

After the fight, Hélio's nephew, Carlson Gracie, wanted to defeat Santana to avenge his uncle. In 1956, Carlson and Santana faced each other at the Maracanãzinho arena with more than 11,000 people in attendance. Carlson got the upper hand and defeated Santana under Vale Tudo rules.

MUHAMMAD ALI VS. ANTONIO INOKI

Legendary boxer Muhammad Ali and catch-wrestler Antonio Inoki agreed to a mixed-rules match billed as "The War of the Worlds." At a press conference alongside the Japanese Amateur Wrestling Association president, Ichiro Hatta, Ali bragged, "Isn't there any [Asian] fighter who will challenge me? I'll give him $1 million if he wins." Inoki accepted Ali's challenge. Financial backers agreed to pay Ali $6 million to fight Inoki.

The match took place on June 26, 1976, in Japan. The rules stated that Inoki could not throw, grapple, or tackle Ali, and he was only permitted to kick if he had one knee on the mat. During the fight, Inoki kicked Ali's legs 107 times while lying on his back. The outcome of the fight was a draw, but this has often been debated.

Although this was a mixed-rules match, it's far from what an MMA fight is like today. While Ali and Inoki were two fighters from different backgrounds and disciplines, the disciplines were not really "mixed." Rather, they were just two

Ichiro Hatta

men being extremely limited in their chosen approaches. However, Inoki's tactic of kicking Ali's legs foreshadowed what would become one of MMA's most effective techniques.

Inoki (*left*) and Ali (*right*) kid around at a press conference before their match.

Kevin Rosier (*top*) and Zane Frazier met in the quarterfinals at the first UFC event.

CHAPTER 4

MMA GOES MAINSTREAM

Mixed martial arts remained a scattering of individual fights until 1993. This was when the Ultimate Fighting Championship (UFC) was established. Finally, MMA had a rough set of rules and a legitimate platform under which to compete.

THE BIRTH OF THE OCTAGON

Art Davie, an American entrepreneur and student of Rorion Gracie, came up with the idea that became the UFC. He proposed that Rorion Gracie and John Milius, an American movie writer and director, hold an eight-man elimination tournament. It would pit fighters of different styles against each other in no-holds-barred combat. He suggested the tournament be called War of the Worlds. The aim was to determine the best and most effective martial art in a

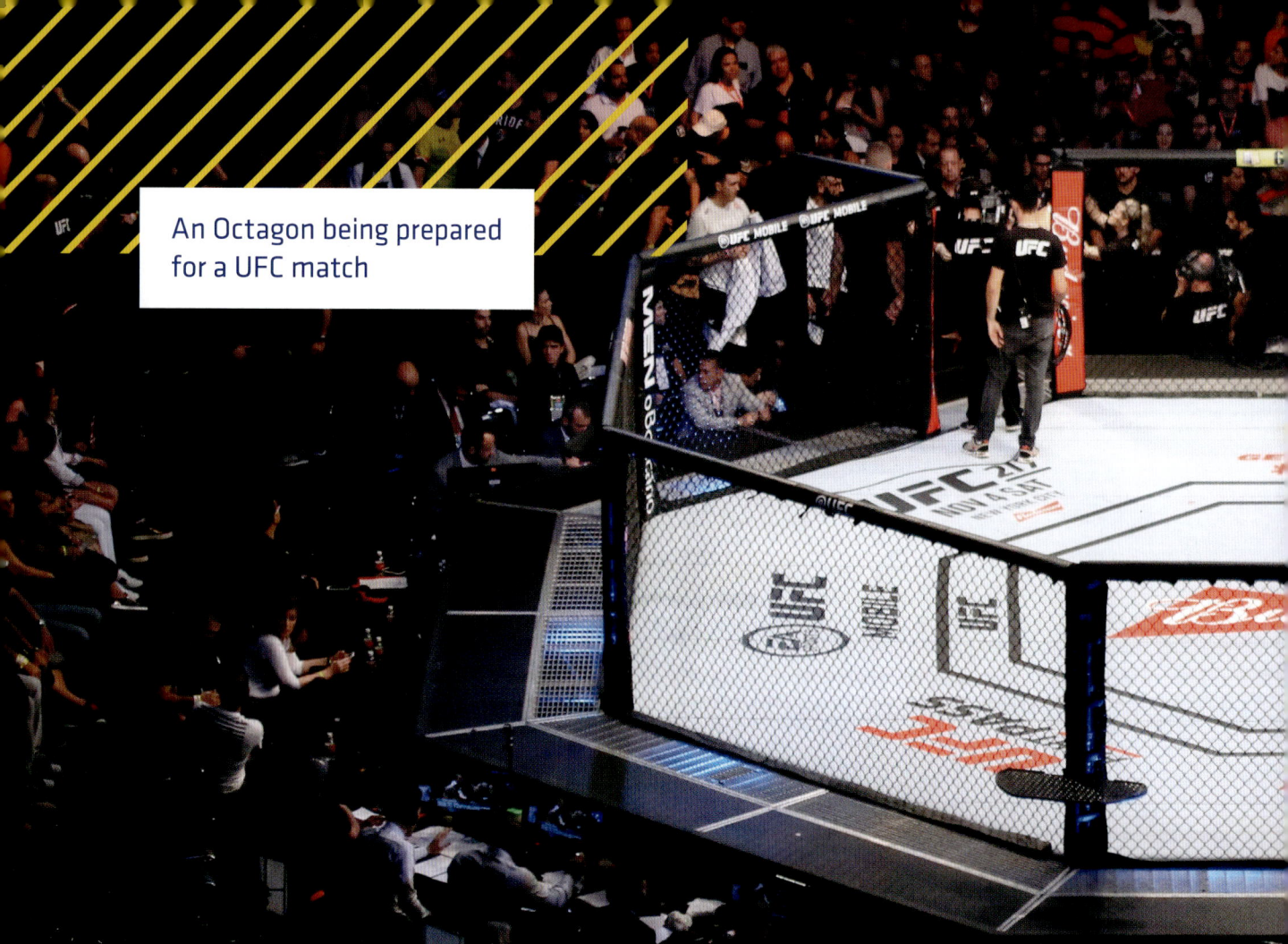

An Octagon being prepared for a UFC match

"real fight." Milius and Gracie agreed and formed the company WOW Promotions to develop the first UFC tournament.

WOW Promotions then partnered with pay-per-view (PPV) company Semaphore Entertainment Group (SEG) to televise the event. SEG hired video and film art director Jason Cusson to design a special ring for the fights. Gracie and Davie had concerns about using a roped ring like in boxing. They thought a fighter could be thrown out of the ring or might leave the ring to gain advantage in grappling exchanges. They and SEG also wanted something visually different from boxing or professional wrestling. In response, Cusson designed the Octagon. It is an eight-sided cage with a chain-link

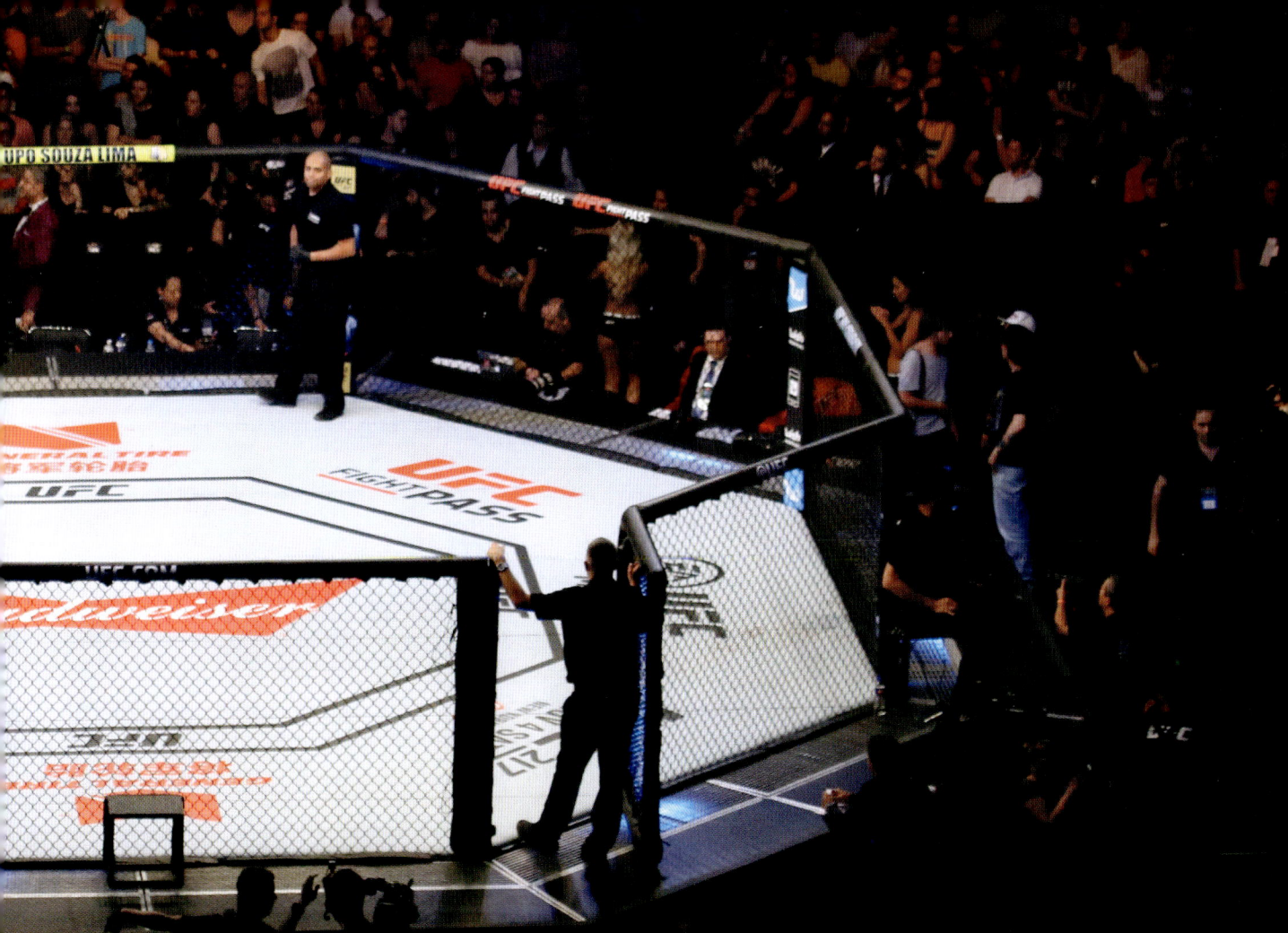

fence and a slightly padded mat. In the UFC, the Octagon is 30 feet (9.1 m) across and 6 feet (1.8 m) tall.

UFC 1

The infamous UFC 1 took place in Denver, Colorado, on November 12, 1993. Art Davie was the matchmaker. The matchmaker's job is to decide who fights whom. UFC 1 featured kickboxers Patrick Smith and Kevin Rosier, savate fighter Gerard Gordeau, karate practitioner Zane Frazier, legendary shootfighter Ken Shamrock, sumo wrestler Teila Tuli, boxer Art Jimmerson, and BJJ practitioner Royce Gracie.

UFC 1 was as close to a "real fight" as you could get. There were no rules, no time limits, no weight classes, and, interestingly, no judges. It was as pure a fight as possible. To win, a fighter would have to knock his opponent out or submit him. Whether this took one minute or 20 minutes, the fight would go on for as long as necessary. Gracie was the eventual winner. He submitted three fighters on his way to victory, in spite of being the smaller man. This proved just how effective BJJ can be.

The tournament was successful. More than 86,000 people viewed it on PPV. However, UFC was slow to become mainstream. A key issue was the lack of rules. In 1996, 36 US states banned no-holds-barred fighting. This limited where the UFC could hold events. So, the UFC

Art Davie

Milius is best known for directing the 1982 movie *Conan the Barbarian*.

There are hundreds of UFC fights every year.

ULTIMATE FIGHTING CHAMPIONSHIP

The Ultimate Fighting Championship is, without a doubt, the premier MMA promotion in the world. Founded in 1993, the UFC would become the first mainstream MMA promotion. Those in the UFC had to deal with the setbacks, aid in rule progression, and be accountable for any early missteps. As the popularity of MMA grew, the UFC created more weight classes in order to make fights safer, fairer, and more competitive. Today, it's widely accepted that UFC champions are the best MMA fighters in the world.

started cooperating with state athletic commissions that make sure athletic events are carried out safely. This led to some unified rules that all UFC fighters must abide by when competing for the organization.

UFC ATTIRE

At UFC 1, there were no specific clothes or equipment that all competitors had to wear. Famously, Art Jimmerson, who fought Royce Gracie in their first-round bout, wore just one boxing glove! Jimmerson believed this would allow the referee to see him tapping out with his non-gloved hand. Royce Gracie wore the traditional *gi* and his black belt. Others also wore clothing traditional for their styles of fighting.

In today's MMA, every fighter must wear four-ounce leather gloves. They also have to wear shorts. Fighters can choose from Vale Tudo shorts, which are skintight, or gladiator shorts, which have a cut down each side. Women have the option of shorts or

Smith holds a photo from his UFC 1 match. He lost to Shamrock.

a skort with either a sports bra or a tight-fitting T-shirt. All competitors must wear gum shields, and male competitors must wear groin guards.

MMA ENDGAME

An MMA fight ends with either a finish or a judges' decision. A finish is when one fighter wins before the end of the rounds. This includes winning by submission, knockout, technical knockout, or disqualification. If neither fighter finishes by the end of the last round, then the winner is determined by the three fight judges. If all three judges choose the same winner, it's called a unanimous decision. If they don't all agree, it's called a split or majority decision. The winner is the fighter chosen by two of the judges.

Jimmerson (*left*) and Gracie during their UFC 1 match

A 2006 Pride FC match between Mark Coleman and Pride FC's heavyweight champion Fedor Emelianenko in Las Vegas, Nevada. It was Pride FC's first event in the United States.

CHAPTER 5

RISE IN POPULARITY

Due to the success of UFC 1, the UFC held more events. There were three to five UFC events a year for the next few years. But the UFC was not the only MMA promotion during these early days of MMA.

PRIDE FIGHTING CHAMPIONSHIPS

UFC was joined by Pride Fighting Championships (Pride FC) in October 1997. This Japan-based promotion was one of the most popular platforms for MMA in the world. Visually, it looked different from the UFC. The fighters competed in a traditional four-sided, roped ring. This proved just how effective the Octagon was, however, as competitors regularly fell out of the ring!

Like early UFC events, Pride FC had a very limited rule set. The promotion allowed soccer kicks to an opponent's head, stomps, and

Takashi Sugiura

spiking, which is lifting an opponent and slamming them headfirst onto the mat. There were also no weight classes. As a result, Pride FC hosted a number of what they called "freak show fights." Often, these events would match up two fighters who were vastly different in size. One of these fights was between Giant Silva, who was over 7 feet (2.1 m) tall and weighed 385 pounds (175 kg), and Takashi Sugiura, who was just under 6 feet (1.8 m) tall and weighed 196 pounds (89 kg). Surprisingly, Sugiura won! Fights like these were what originally made Pride FC so memorable.

PRIDE FC TOURNAMENTS

Pride FC is especially known for its single-elimination tournaments. The openweight tournament that was held on May 1, 2000, would go down in history as one of the most competitive events in MMA history. With the quarterfinals, semifinals, and final all being held on the same evening, the event was packed with world-class talent. The eventual winner, Mark Coleman, had become the first-ever UFC heavyweight champion at UFC 12 in February 1997. Coleman was a Pan-American wrestling champion who used his wrestling skills to dominate fights and punish his opponents. The 2000 openweight

Coleman was inducted into the UFC Hall of Fame in 2008.

Silva (*left*) and Hidehiko Yoshida in their semifinal bout at the 2003 Pride FC Grand Prix in Tokyo, Japan. Silva defeated Yoshida and went on to win the championship.

tournament also included big names such as Royce Gracie, Kazushi Sakuraba, Igor Vovchanchyn, and Mark Kerr. They all went on to become legends of the sport.

In 2003, Pride FC held a middleweight grand prix tournament. Wanderlei Silva won, defeating Quinton Jackson in the final. Silva was notorious for never backing down from a fight and having brutal knockout power. He holds Pride FC's record for the most wins, knockouts, and title defenses, and the longest winning streak.

ZUFFA'S TAKEOVER OF THE UFC

While Pride FC was operating in Japan, the UFC was undergoing changes in the United States. In 1995, SEG bought the UFC from WOW Promotions. Six years later, SEG sold it to Las Vegas production company Zuffa. Zuffa is operated by casino owners Frank and Lorenzo Fertitta and the Fertittas' business partner, Dana White. Zuffa's ownership of the UFC was vital around this time. Lorenzo was a former member of the Nevada State Athletic Commission and was able to secure sanctioning for the UFC in Nevada in 2001. Since then, the UFC has been based in Las Vegas.

(left to right) Frank Fertitta, White, Lorenzo Fertitta

With the purchase by Zuffa, the UFC's popularity increased. Zuffa was able to get more advertising, which drew more viewers. The UFC continued to be available exclusively through PPV until 2002. That's when the UFC secured its first cable television deal with Fox Sports Net. Initially, the network mainly aired hour-long highlights featuring the best fights from past UFC events. This cable network exposure attracted more new fans.

UFC 40 was an important event in the Zuffa era of the UFC. It took place at MGM Grand Arena in Las Vegas on November 22, 2002. More than 13,000 people attended and 150,000 watched

Tito Ortiz (right) lands a right on Shamrock during the UFC 40 heavyweight title fight. Ortiz won in three rounds.

Chuck Liddell

on PPV. Stacked with two title fights as well as two future legends and a former welterweight champion, the fight card delivered on a huge scale.

Tito Ortiz defeated UFC 1 veteran Ken Shamrock in the main event. Future UFC Hall of Famer Chuck Liddell knocked out Renato Sobral, and Matt Hughes finished Gil Castillo for the welterweight championship. Legendary MMA referee John McCarthy referred to UFC 40 as the turning point for MMA. He said that when he stood in the Octagon for the main event, that's when he honestly believed MMA would make it as a sport.

In 2007, Frank and Lorenzo Fertitta bought Pride FC for $65 million. Dana White announced that the UFC would bring in Pride FC's biggest names. Pride FC officially closed its Japanese office in October 2007, with many of its fighters signing for different promotions.

John McCarthy

THE ULTIMATE FIGHTER

Another turning point for the UFC, and MMA in general, was the reality television series *The Ultimate Fighter*. In spite of the UFC's popularity, it wasn't progressing the way the Fertittas and White predicted. By 2004, the owners had lost $34 million since their purchase. With financial worries, they stepped away from the PPV model and developed their own reality series.

The Ultimate Fighter began in 2005. It aired on Spike TV, following *WWE Raw*. The hope was that World Wrestling Entertainment (WWE) fans would continue watching the channel and become MMA fans. Following the successes of the first *The Ultimate Fighter* season, a second was launched seven months later, with two more seasons in 2006. The show continued with two seasons each year. The thirtieth season aired in 2022.

Several fighters who won on *The Ultimate Fighter* have gone on to win UFC titles. These include England's Michael Bisping and Australia's Robert Whittaker, who both captured the middleweight belt. Most famous of all was American fighter Matt Serra, who won the welterweight belt in one of the biggest upsets in UFC history.

Bisping is also an actor. He is in the 2017 spy movie *XXX: Return of Xander Cage*.

In 2008, Mike Brown (*left*) defeated Urijah Faber for the WEC featherweight world title.

CHAPTER 6

PROMOTION FUSION

The UFC and Pride FC were joined by World Extreme Cagefighting (WEC) in 2001. These were the three premier MMA promotions during the early 2000s. Although they weren't the only ones, these three had the biggest names, the best fights, and the most fans. But further changes were in store for MMA.

WORLD EXTREME CAGEFIGHTING

When WEC started, it had numerous weight classes. But it was most famous for its lighter weight classes. These were bantamweight (135 pounds / 61.2 kg), featherweight (145 pounds / 65.8 kg) and lightweight (155 pounds / 70.3 kg). The Fertittas realized the value of WEC, so Zuffa purchased it in December 2006.

WEC's focus on lighter classes complemented the UFC, which focused more on heavier classes.

Aldo (*foreground*) and Mendes fought each other twice for the featherweight championship. Aldo won both fights.

WEC gave legendary fighters including José Aldo, Dominick Cruz, and Urijah Faber a platform to showcase their skill where the UFC didn't. But lighter classes proved to have more popular fighters. In 2008, WEC started phasing out the heavier weight classes.

In December 2010, Zuffa merged WEC with the UFC. Most WEC fighters were transferred to the UFC. Legendary WEC fighters

Aldo (*left*) is considered by many to be the best featherweight mixed martial artist of all time.

including Aldo, Benson Henderson, Anthony Pettis, and Chad Mendes soon became well-known figures in the UFC.

STRIKEFORCE

In addition to WEC, the UFC also owes a lot to Strikeforce. Strikeforce was a US-based promotion run by longtime promoter Scott Coker. It was founded in 1985 and initially focused exclusively on kickboxing. Strikeforce started producing MMA events in March 2006.

Following early successes, Strikeforce partnered with television network NBC in 2008 to televise fights. This exposure helped Strikeforce sign some big names in the MMA scene. Notably, Nick Diaz, Jake Shields, and Robbie Lawler signed

Coker *right*) has loved martial arts all his life. He is known for his ability to anticipate new trends in the sport.

contracts with Strikeforce. These fighters all came to Strikeforce from EliteXC, a short-lived MMA promotion in Los Angeles, California. The partnership with NBC also led to partnerships with Japanese promotion DREAM and Russian promotion M-1 Global.

Ronaldo Souza (*left*) retired from MMA in 2021.

This allowed for cross-promotion fights. It also allowed fighters to really test themselves against a wider range of opponents.

Strikeforce brought back MMA grand prix tournaments, which had been discontinued following the UFC's purchase of Pride FC. The men's heavyweight grand prix tournament was contested between February 2011 and May 2012. The winner was future two-weight UFC world champion Daniel Cormier. The men's middleweight and women's bantamweight grand prix were each contested in just one night. These tournaments were won by Jorge Santiago and Miesha Tate, respectively. Tate would go on to become the UFC bantamweight champion in 2016.

About 320,000 people tuned in to watch Strikeforce Challengers 13 in 2011.

In 2011, Strikeforce, like WEC before it, was purchased by Zuffa. White announced that Strikeforce would continue as its own independent promotion and that Scott Coker would continue to lead it. Strikeforce held tournaments and other events for two more years. Strikeforce held its final event in January 2013. Then, all fighter contracts were either canceled or transferred to the UFC.

Cormier retired in 2020. He then became a commentator for the UFC.

Cris Cyborg is the only MMA fighter to win championships in the Bellator, Strikeforce, Invicta, and UFC promotions.

As of 2022, Patrício "Pitbull" Freire has won 21 Bellator fights, the most of any fighter within the promotion.

BELLATOR

Scott Coker's run with Strikeforce came to an end in 2013 when it merged with the UFC. In 2014, Coker took control of Bellator MMA, a world-renowned promotion created in 2008 by Bjorn Rebney. Under Rebney, Bellator held single-elimination tournaments where the winner received $100,000 and was guaranteed a world title fight. When Coker took over, he changed the format to the more common single-fight event schedule. Bellator also holds occasional grand prix tournaments.

Often when a UFC fighter's contract ends, they will choose to sign with Bellator. Bellator is known for giving fighters higher pay-per-fight contracts, which can be a big draw

MMA ALL-STAR
RONDA ROUSEY

Ronda Rousey was born in 1987 in Riverside, California. She started out in judo, winning a bronze medal at the 2008 Olympic Games in Beijing, China. She switched to MMA in 2011 and signed with Strikeforce. Rousey was the women's bantamweight champion in Strikeforce and later in the UFC. She is considered one of the greatest women's champions of all time, winning 12 straight fights by either knockout or submission. Rousey retired from MMA in 2016. Two years later she became the first woman inducted into the UFC Hall of Fame.

In 2015, Rousey (*right*) knocked out Brazilian fighter Bethe Correia in 34 seconds.

for some fighters. Notable names to cross over from the UFC to Bellator in their primes include Gegard Mousasi, Ryan Bader, Sergio Pettis, and Cris Cyborg. They all became Bellator champions.

ALTERNATIVE PROMOTIONS

There is no doubt that the UFC is the number one MMA promotion in the world. It has the best fighters, the most eyes on its events, the biggest names, and the most money. Bellator is widely seen as the number two promotion, but others are giving it some serious competition.

The Professional Fighters League (PFL) was founded in 2018 by Donn Davis. It is the first major promotion where athletes compete in a regular season, post-season, and championship rather than competing consistently throughout the year. The top four fighters from these seasons are entered into the playoffs. The winner of the tournament will not only become the PFL season champion but also receive $1 million in prize money. The PFL is making waves in the sport. It could become one of the world's biggest and most well-regarded promotions.

ONE Championship is also a popular promotion, especially in

Davis modeled the PFL on other sports leagues, such as those in basketball and soccer.

The 2021 PFL World Championship took place in Hollywood, Florida. It featured ten fights, including one between Omari Akhmedov and Jordan Young.

Asia. It was created in 2011 by entrepreneur Chatri Sityodtong and former ESPN Star Sports senior executive Victor Cui. Based out of Singapore, ONE Championship events often feature a mix of combat sports events, with the same fight card featuring MMA bouts, Muay Thai bouts, kickboxing, and submission grappling matches. ONE is enticing for fighters due to better pay and safer

51

Yamato Fujita (*left*) kicks Mitsuhisa Sunabe in the head during their semifinal bout at the Rizin Fighting World Grand Prix 2017.

weight-cutting regulations. Most famously, Demetrious Johnson, former UFC champion and one of the best MMA fighters in history, signed with ONE in 2018.

Other up-and-coming MMA promotions include Cage Warriors, Legacy Fighting Alliance, Konfrontacja Sztuk Walki, Pancrase, Invicta Fighting Championships, Rizin Fighting Federation, and AMC Fight Nights. Each of these promotions influences the MMA game in its own way. For now, they serve an important role as feeder promotions for the UFC and Bellator. Often, if a fighter proves themself in one of the smaller promotions, one of the big two will offer them a contract.

Shannon Knapp founded Invicta Fighting Championships in 2012. She was inducted into the International Sports Hall of Fame in 2022.

Shinya Aoki began fighting with ONE Championship in 2012.

McGregor is known for taunting other fighters at prefight press conferences.

CHAPTER 7

WHAT THE FUTURE HOLDS

The world of MMA continues to evolve. In 2012, the International Mixed Martial Arts Federation (IMMAF) was founded. It provides regulation, oversight, and support for MMA around the world. It helps countries develop their own MMA programs and national federations. The goal of the IMMAF is to ensure the sport will become safer, as well as continue to grow and attract exciting new fighters.

RISING STARS

Some recent fighters to rise to the top include Conor McGregor, Jorge Masvidal, and Israel Adesanya. These three men have changed the game through their fighting styles as well as their conduct outside of the Octagon. This includes trash talk and social media interactions.

Brazilian fighter Amanda Nunes was the first woman to become a double champion.

McGregor, for example, is one of the biggest stars MMA has ever produced. Maybe it's his exciting knockout fighting style. Maybe it's that he's from Ireland, where few world-class fighters have come from. Or maybe he simply rose into the spotlight at the right time. Whatever it is, he has taken MMA by storm.

DOUBLE CHAMPIONS

A double champion is a fighter who is the champion of two different weight classes at the same time. There have only been seven double champions in the UFC. But there will likely be more fighters attempting this achievement in the future. One reason for this is that MMA fighters average two or three fights per year. This means there can be several months between fights. Their weight can change during this time, putting them in a different class. The challenge is whether they can be as good in the new class as their previous one. Only the best can accomplish it.

The Money Fight was watched by 50 million people in the United States.

MCGREGOR VS. MAYWEATHER

In 2017, Conor McGregor (*above right*) took on Floyd Mayweather Jr. in a boxing match. It was referred to as the Money Fight. Mayweather had a legendary boxing career, with 49 wins and zero losses and 15 major world championships. Mayweather's boxing skills ultimately led him to a victory in ten rounds. After the fight, McGregor claimed that he would be able to use what he learned about Mayweather's fighting style during the fight to defeat him in a rematch.

American MMA star Stephen Thompson regularly posts martial arts tutorials on YouTube. He has more than 400,000 subscribers.

SOCIAL MEDIA

The rise of social media has played a big role in MMA. Fighters regularly call each other out on social media. They have arguments and offer to fight one another on platforms such as Instagram and Twitter. This gets fans excited, allows fighters to hype a potential fight, and makes the matchmakers aware that two fighters are keen to fight one another.

AN EXCITING FUTURE

Going forward, MMA will continue to grow as a sport. In October 2018, a fight between Conor McGregor and Khabib Nurmagomedov brought in a record 2,400,000

Like McGregor (*not pictured*), Ian Garry (*left*) is an Irish MMA fighter. He is a rising star in the sport.

PPV buys. More breakout stars like McGregor will be entering the Octagon, and more promotions will likely rise to compete with the UFC and Bellator. If the past is any indicator, the future of MMA will be full of exciting surprises.

TIMELINE

648 BCE
Pankration begins as an Olympic sport in ancient Greece.

1917
Carlos Gracie learns judo and jiu-jitsu from Mitsuyo Maeda. Gracie and his brothers develop their own style of MMA called Brazilian Jiu-jitsu.

1976
Boxer Muhammad Ali and wrestler Antonio Inoki fight one of the first mixed-rules matches.

1882 CE
In Japan, Jigorō Kanō uses elements of jiu-jitsu to form a new martial art called judo.

1960s
Bruce Lee develops a style of MMA called Jeet Kune Do. He popularizes MMA through his movies.

1993
The Ultimate Fighting Championship (UFC) is established.

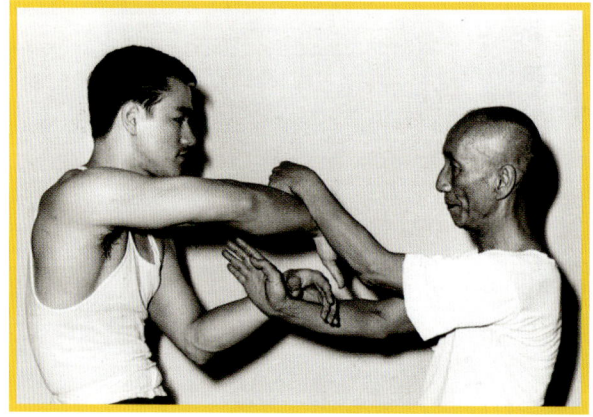

1997 — Pride Fighting Championships (Pride FC) is established.

2001 — The Fertitta brothers and Dana White purchase the UFC through their production company Zuffa. They move the headquarters to Las Vegas, Nevada.

2005 — *The Ultimate Fighter 1* airs on Spike TV.

2006 — Zuffa purchases World Extreme Cagefighting.

2011 — Zuffa purchases Strikeforce.

2012 — The International Mixed Martial Arts Federation is founded.

2014 — Scott Coker takes over and revitalizes Bellator.

2018 — Donn Davis founds the Professional Fighters League.

GLOSSARY

breakout—an achievement that is significantly better than previous efforts.

catch wrestling—a form of wrestling developed in England in the 1800s that combines several wrestling styles.

complement—to go well with or complete something.

consistently—in a way that continues to develop or happen in the same way.

debate—a discussion or an argument.

entrepreneur—one who organizes, manages, and accepts the risks of a business or an enterprise.

eye-gouging—pushing one's thumb or fingers into someone's eye.

federation—a union of organizations that have the same or a similar purpose.

finale—an important or exciting last display in an event.

foreshadow—to give a hint of beforehand.

gi—the traditional robe worn by people who practice martial arts such as judo and karate.

gladiator—a person who fought to the death for public entertainment in ancient Rome.

hand-to-hand—a fight between two people that may involve weapons such as knives.

hype—promotional publicity designed to create excitement about something.

induct—to admit as a member.

infamous—having a bad reputation.

mainstream—the ideas, attitudes, activities, or trends that are regarded as normal or dominant in society.

manipulate—to treat or operate in a skillful way.

notorious—having a widely known and usually negative reputation.

Pan-American—relating to or involving the independent republics of North and South America.

potential—something that can occur or be achieved in the future.

practitioner—one who practices a certain profession, sport, or craft.

potential—something that can occur or be achieved in the future.

promotion—an organization or company that organizes MMA fights and tournaments.

screenwriter—a person who writes the story and directions for a movie.

single-elimination—a tournament format in which a player or team has to win every game or match to stay in the tournament.

stamina—the power to endure fatigue, disease, or hardship.

weight cutting—the practice of quickly losing weight before competing in a sport such as MMA, wrestling, or boxing.

ONLINE RESOURCES

To learn more about MMA history, please visit **abdobooklinks.com** or scan this QR code. These links are routinely monitored and updated to provide the most current information available.

INDEX

Adesanya, Israel, 55
Aldo, José, 44-45
Ali, Muhammad, 22-23
AMC Fight Nights, 53

Bader, Ryan, 50
Bellator MMA, 48, 50, 53, 59
Bisping, Michael, 41
Bonnar, Stephan, 5-7

Cage Warriors, 53
Castillo, Gil, 40
clothing, 9, 11, 30-31
Coker, Scott, 45, 47-48
Coleman, Mark, 35
Cormier, Daniel, 46
Cruz, Dominick, 44
Cui, Victor, 51
Cusson, Jason, 26
Cyborg, Cris, 50

Davie, Art, 25-27
Davis, Donn, 50
Diaz, Nick, 45
DREAM, 45

EliteXC, 45

Faber, Urijah, 44
Fertitta, Frank, 37, 40-41, 43
Fertitta, Lorenzo, 37, 40-41, 43
fighting styles, 9, 11-12, 14-16, 20, 22, 25-28, 30, 35, 45, 49, 51, 57
Frazier, Zane, 27

Gordeau, Gerard, 27
Gracie, Carlos, 12, 19-20
Gracie, Carlson, 22
Gracie, Hélio, 12, 19-20, 22
Gracie, Rorion, 25-26
Gracie, Royce, 27-28, 30, 36
Gracie Challenges, 15, 19
Gracie family, 12, 14-15, 19
Griffin, Forrest, 5-7

Hatta, Ichiro, 22
Henderson, Benson, 45
Hughes, Matt, 40

Inoki, Antonio, 22-23

International Mixed Martial Arts Federation (IMMAF), 55
Invicta Fighting Championships, 53

Jackson, Quinton, 36
Japanese Amateur Wrestling Association, 22
Jimmerson, Art, 27, 30
Johnson, Demetrious, 53

Kanō, Jigorō, 11
Kerr, Mark, 36
Kimura, Masahiko, 19-20
Konfrontacja Sztuk Walki, 53

Lawler, Robbie, 45
Lee, Bruce, 15-16
Legacy Fighting Alliance, 53
Liddell, Chuck, 40

M-1 Global, 45
Maeda, Mitsuyo, 11-12
Masvidal, Jorge, 55
Mayweather, Floyd, Jr., 57
McCarthy, John, 40
McGregor, Conor, 55-59
Mendes, Chad, 45
Milius, John, 25-26
Mousasi, Gegard, 50
movie industry, 15-16, 25-26

Nevada State Athletic Commission, 37
Nurmagomedov, Khabib, 58

Octagon, 25-27, 33, 40, 55, 59
Olympic Games, 9, 49
ONE Championship, 50-51, 53
Ortiz, Tito, 40

Pancrase, 53
pankration, 9
pay-per-view (PPV), 26, 28, 38, 40-41, 59
Pettis, Anthony, 45
Pettis, Sergio, 50
Pride Fighting Championships (Pride FC), 33, 35-37, 40, 43, 46
Professional Fighters League (PFL), 50

Rebney, Bjorn, 48
Rizin Fighting Federation, 53
Rogan, Joe, 6
Rosier, Kevin, 27
Rousey, Ronda, 49
rules, 9, 22, 25, 28-30, 33

Sakuraba, Kazushi, 36
Santana, Valdemar, 20, 22
Santiago, Jorge, 46
Semaphore Entertainment Group (SEG), 26, 37
Serra, Matt, 4
Shamrock, Ken, 27, 40
Shields, Jake, 45
Silva, Giant, 35
Silva, Wanderlei, 36
Sityodtong, Chatri, 51
Smith, Patrick, 27
Sobral, Renato, 40
social media, 55, 58
Strikeforce, 45-49
Sugiura, Takashi, 35

Tate, Miesha, 46
television networks, 5, 38, 41, 45, 51
tournaments, 25-26, 28, 35-36, 46-48, 50
Tuli, Teila, 27

UFC Hall of Fame, 40, 49
Ultimate Fighter, The, 5, 7, 41
Ultimate Fighting Championship (UFC), 5, 7, 16, 25-30, 33, 35, 37-38, 40-41, 43-50, 53, 56, 59

Vovchanchyn, Igor, 36

weight classes, 28, 35-36, 40-41, 43-44, 46, 49, 56
White, Dana, 5, 7, 16, 37, 40-41, 47
Whittaker, Robert, 41
World Extreme Cagefighting (WEC), 43-45, 47
World Wrestling Entertainment (WWE), 41
WOW Promotions, 26, 37

Zuffa, 37-38, 43-44, 47